MW01436525

WHITMAN
MIDDLE SCHOOL LIBRARY
SEATTLE

DEMCO

Science Links

Amusement Park SCIENCE

Dan Greenberg

CHELSEA CLUBHOUSE
An Imprint of Chelsea House Publishers
A Haights Cross Communications Company
Philadelphia

This edition first published in 2003 by Chelsea Clubhouse, a division of
Chelsea House Publishers and a subsidiary of Haights Cross Communications.

A Haights Cross Communications Company

This edition was adapted from Newbridge Discovery Links® by arrangement with Newbridge Educational Publishing. All rights reserved. No part of this publication may be reproduced or transmitted in any form or by any means without the written permission of the publisher. Printed and bound in the United States of America.

Chelsea Clubhouse
1974 Sproul Road, Suite 400
Broomall, PA 19008-0914

The Chelsea House world wide web address is www.chelseahouse.com

Library of Congress Cataloging-in-Publication Data
Greenberg, Daniel A.
  Amusement park science / by Dan Greenberg.
     p. cm. — (Science links)
Includes index.
Welcome to the amusement park — On a collision course: bumper cars — Round and round: carousels and Ferris wheels — In the swing: pendulum rides — The biggest thrill: roller coasters — More forces at play.
ISBN 0-7910-7416-1
1. Physics—Juvenile literature. 2. Amusement parks—Juvenile literature. [1. Physics.
2. Amusement parks.] I. Title. II. Series.
  QC25 .G74 2003
  531—dc21

2002015893

Copyright © Newbridge Educational Publishing LLC

Newbridge Discovery Links Guided Reading Program Author: Dr. Brenda Parkes
Content Reviewer: Professor Louis A. Bloomfield, Department of Physics, University of Virginia
Written by Dan Greenberg

Cover Photograph: Double-loop roller coaster
Table of Contents Photograph: Children on roller coaster

Photo Credits:
Cover: Lester Lefkowitz/The Stock Market/CORBIS; Contents page: Tom & DeAnn McCarthy/The Stock Market/CORBIS; Pages 4–5: Kelly-Mooney Photography/CORBIS; Pages 6–7: Eunice Harris/Photo Researchers; Page 8: Ann Purcell/Photo Researchers, Inc.; Page 9: (top) Bettmann/CORBIS, (bottom) Karl Weatherly/CORBIS; Pages 10–11: Alan Schein/The Stock Market/CORBIS; Page 12: John Henley/The Stock Market/CORBIS; Page 13: Wolfgang Kaehler/CORBIS; Page 14: (background) Joseph Sohm, ChromoSohm, Inc./CORBIS, (inset) Lawrence Migdale/Photo Researchers, Inc.; Page 15: Tom & DeAnn McCarthy/The Stock Market/CORBIS; Page 16: Rafael Macia/Photo Researchers, Inc.; Page 17: Rafael Macia/Photo Researchers, Inc.; Page 18: Charles Krebs/The Stock Market/CORBIS; Page 19: Charles D. Winters/Photo Researchers, Inc.; Page 20: Jeffrey W. Myers/CORBIS; Pages 20–21: Andrew J. G. Bell, Eye Ubiquitous/CORBIS; Page 22: Tom & DeAnn McCarthy/The Stock Market/CORBIS; Page 24: Karl Weatherly/CORBIS; Page 25: Rafael Macia/Photo Researchers, Inc.; Page 26: Adam Wolfitt/CORBIS; Page 27: Mike Chew/The Stock Market/CORBIS; Page 28: (top) Mary Ellen Meyer/The Stock Market/CORBIS, (bottom) Kevin Daly/The Stock Market/CORBIS; Page 29: (top) Alan Schein/The Stock Market/CORBIS, (bottom) Nathan Benn/CORBIS

Maps/Illustrations by Sidney Jablonski, Pages 13, 23

While every care has been taken to trace and acknowledge photo copyrights for this edition, the publisher apologizes for any accidental infringement where copyright has proved untraceable.
Melville

Table of Contents

Welcome to the Amusement Park 4

On a Collision Course: Bumper Cars 6

Round and Round:
Carousels and Ferris Wheels 10

In the Swing: Pendulum Rides 16

The Biggest Thrill: Roller Coasters 20

More Forces at Play 28

Websites 30

Glossary 31

Index 32

According to the National Consumer Product Safety Commission, amusement park rides are among the safest forms of recreation. You're safer atop the Ferris wheel or hurtling down the hills of a roller coaster than you are riding a bike or playing ball.

Welcome
to the Amusement Park

Come on in. Take a look around. The amusement park is filled with music and swirling lights. But mostly it's a place to experience the thrill of motion.

As the rides twirl and spin, climb and dip, passengers giggle and squeal. As the rides lurch and plunge, passengers shout and scream at the top of their lungs. What's all the fuss about?

Amusement park rides provide thrills, but they also keep you sitting safely in your seat. Rides can do this because they are objects, and all objects follow a few simple physical laws when they move. To find out how your favorite rides put these laws into action, just turn the page!

On a Collision Course: Bumper Cars

Hey, watch out! If you're not careful, you could end up . . . **POW! SMASH! BAM!** . . . crashing into somebody!

Not to worry. Bumper cars, you see, are not like other cars. With normal cars, the object is to avoid accidents. With bumper cars, the object is to **RAM**, **JAM**, and **SLAM** into anything that moves!

As soon as your car is hit, it's likely to be sent spinning off into another direction. Meanwhile, inside of the bumper car, you bounce backward and forward, right and left. What's the reason for all of this knocking around?

It's easy to see how bumper cars got their name. The wide bumper around the bottom of each car ensures that the cars and the passengers get fairly gentle jolts each time they collide.

A Moving Experience

Bumper cars do have pedals and steering wheels. But, as long as you keep slamming into other bumper cars, and they keep crashing into you, you don't have complete control.

When two bumper cars collide, they exert forces on each other. A **force** is a push or pull acting on an object.

This boy just rammed into his older sister's car. Each car exerted a force on the other. The impact of the collision caused both cars to shoot backward, away from each other. But, because the boy is smaller and lighter than his sister, his car moved back faster and farther than her car.

Of course, not all bumper car collisions are head-on. Your car is sure to get hit on the sides and in the back, too. But, in any collision, the lighter person is always going to

What would a bumper car ride be like if the cars didn't have steering wheels?

What Did Newton Know About Bumper Cars?

The great scientist Sir Isaac Newton (1642–1727) was the first to explain and write down the laws of motion. **Newton's third law of motion** states that for every action, there is an equal and opposite **reaction**. When the boy's bumper car hit his sister's bumper car, the two cars exerted forces on each other. The forces exerted by the cars were exactly equal in amount but opposite in direction.

feel the greater jolt. Keep this in mind when you make your way around the bumper car course. If the guy rushing toward you is much larger than you, you may want to get out of his way. Otherwise, you might wind up spinning out of control!

Whew! Let's move on to the next ride where you'll see more laws of motion in action.

Forces at Play

You put the laws of motion into action whenever you play tennis. The racket and the ball exert forces on each other that are equal in amount but opposite in direction. The force that the racket exerts on the ball turns the ball around and sends it back over the net.

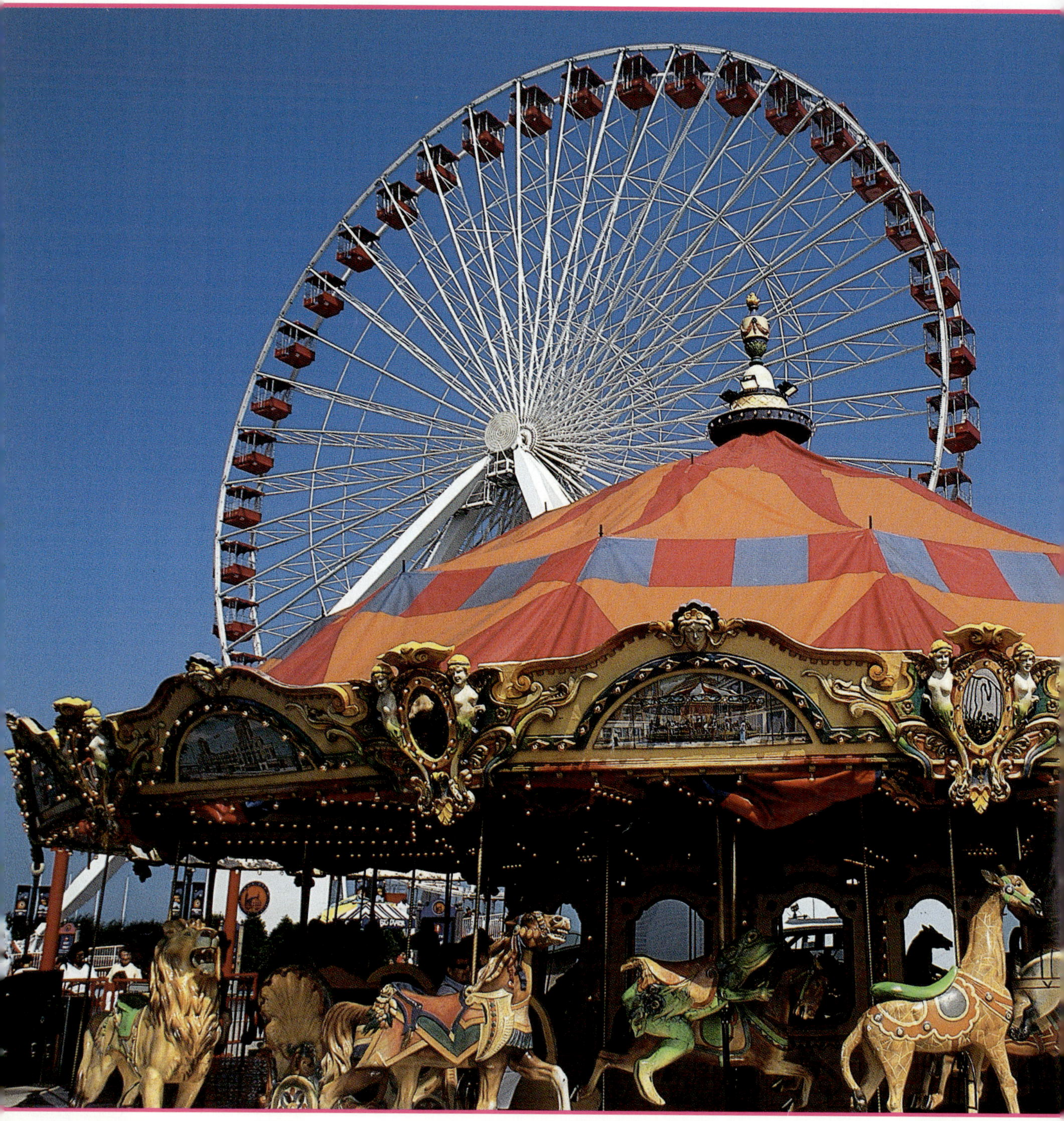

Round and Round: Carousels and Ferris Wheels

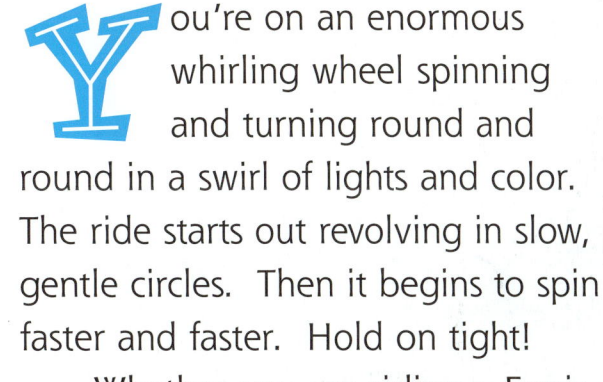

You're on an enormous whirling wheel spinning and turning round and round in a swirl of lights and color. The ride starts out revolving in slow, gentle circles. Then it begins to spin faster and faster. Hold on tight!

Whether you are riding a Ferris wheel or a carousel, you will spin around and around without flying off the ride. On both rides, you travel in a circular path around a central point. Because of this, both rides demonstrate some of the same laws of motion.

Ferris wheels and carousels have been popular attractions for more than 100 years.

Hang on to Your Horse!

Remember the first time you rode on a carousel? Perhaps someone had to help you climb up on your horse, fasten your seat belt, and slip your feet into the stirrups. As you began to travel round and round, you were probably told to hold on tightly to your horse.

Actually, as long as you hold on to some part of the carousel, it will keep you moving around and around in a circular motion. This is because the carousel exerts a **centripetal force** on your body. A centripetal force is a force toward the center of a circle. On a carousel, the centripetal force is toward the center of the carousel itself. The force bends your path into a circle.

The poles on the carousel are attached to the spinning circular platform and canopy. How does this keep the horses spinning?

Where Are the Fastest Horses on a Carousel?

All of the horses on a carousel are bolted onto the same **rotating** platform, but the horses nearest the outside travel the fastest. How could some of them be moving faster than the others?

Imagine that the horses shown below travel on two separate disks. The distance around the outer disk is much greater than the distance around the inner disk. Since all the horses make a complete circle in the same amount of time, the outer horses must move at a faster speed to cover the additional distance.

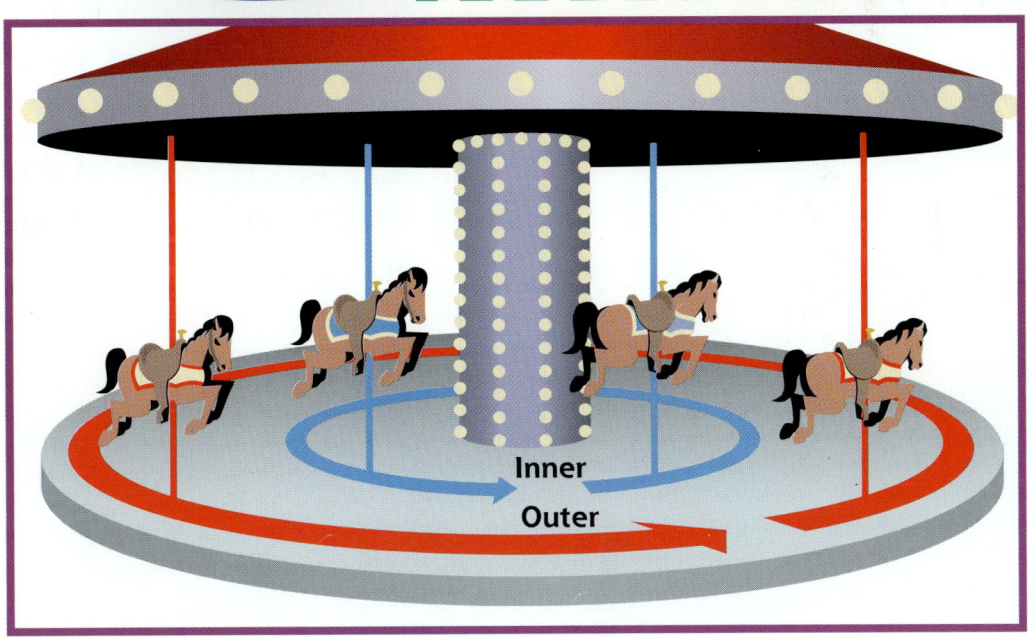

Inner
Outer

Bicycle wheels inspired the inventor George Ferris. He designed a huge ride in which passengers rode in large closed cars. Today, many Ferris wheels use open chairs rather than closed cars. The passengers swing back and forth, so chairs have sturdy bars that keep passengers safely seated.

The Highs and Lows of the Ferris Wheel

A Ferris wheel looks something like a carousel turned on its side. A centripetal force also bends your path into a circle when you ride a Ferris wheel. However, where you sit on a carousel can make a difference in how fast you are moving. On a Ferris wheel, all riders travel at the same speed. But because of the heights you reach, it's likely that you'll find this ride more exciting than a whirl on a carousel.

As the ride spins, you go up, up, UP. When the wheel has turned halfway around, you are up as high as you can get in the amusement park. What a view!

All too soon, you're back at ground level. This ride is over, but there's still more to come.

Forces at Play

This spinning basketball is another example of motion about a central point. This motion also involves a centripetal force. Why does the outer part of the ball spin faster than the inner part that rests on the boy's finger?

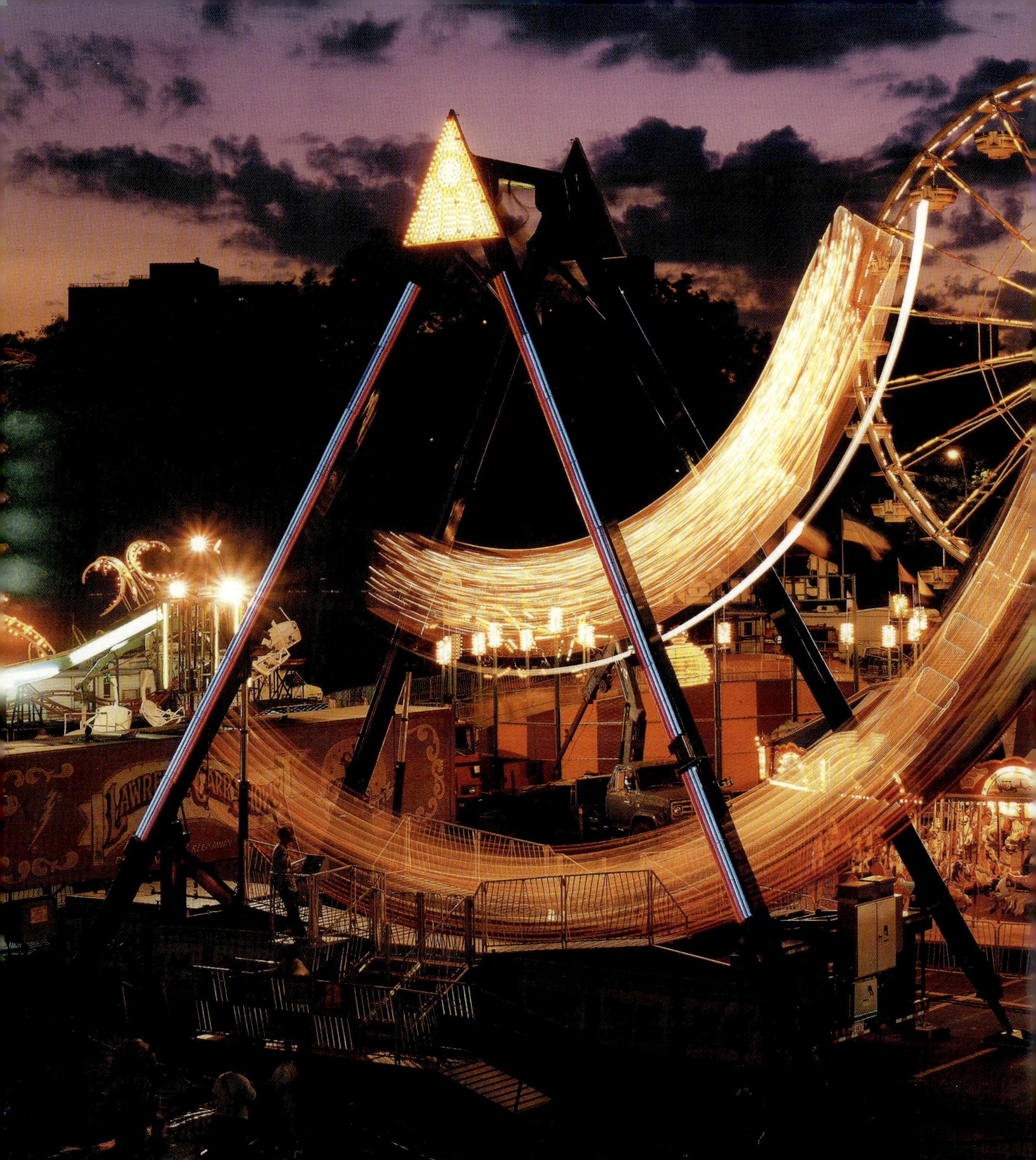

In the Swing: Pendulum Rides

Are you ready to whoosh back and forth and back and forth at higher and higher speeds? If you are, get ready for a ride on the pendulum. Compared to the pendulum, the bumper cars, carousel, and Ferris wheel might seem tame.

As long as the pendulum ride doesn't tip too high, it always takes about the same amount of time to make one full swing. What does this mean for you, the rider? It means that as the pendulum begins to swing higher and higher, it will also begin to swing faster.

Compare the photos of the ride at rest and the ride in full swing. Why do you see two arcs of moving lights in the larger picture?

How High Can You Go?

Pendulum rides use metal cables or beams to support the car in which passengers ride. The supports attach to the central point at the top of the triangle-shaped frame of the ride. The longer the supports, the higher the pendulum can swing, and the more exciting the ride becomes.

Rocking Sensations

Climb aboard and choose your seat. Did you notice that the car for this ride is decorated to look like an ancient ship? As soon as the ride begins, you'll understand why.

The ride sways back and forth, going higher and higher and faster and faster, taking about the same amount of time to complete each back-and-forth swing. This swaying makes some passengers feel as if they are riding the waves of a stormy sea. As the ride rocks higher and higher, the contents of your stomach slosh around. The swaying of the ride also affects the fluid in your inner ear. Some people can easily adjust to these odd sensations, but others end up with a nasty case of motion sickness.

Of course, a pendulum ride offers a more pleasant sensation, too. Some riders thrill at the floating feeling they get when the ride reaches its highest point. It's a feeling of near-weightlessness, the same kind of sensation astronauts experience as they move up into space. This occurs because of the combination of forces acting on the ride and on your body. Where else can you experience weightlessness? You'll find out now that it's time to try the last ride.

Forces at Play

Tick! Tock! The length of the pendulum rod in a clock determines how long each swing will take.

The Biggest Thrill: Roller Coasters

Slowly, ever so slowly, the roller coaster begins to creep up that first impossibly steep hill. The higher you go, the slower the car seems to move. At the very top, you seem to pause for a brief moment some 500 feet (152 meters) above the ground.

Then you feel strangely weightless as you fall, hurtling, crashing, and diving to the bottom at an alarming rate of speed—screaming all the way.

But wait! The ride is just beginning. There are more hills and surprises ahead. One of the biggest surprises of all is what keeps the roller coaster moving through the rest of this wild ride.

Many coasters, like this one, travel on steel tracks. But some roller coaster fans prefer the bumpy ride they get when careening along on an old-fashioned wooden-tracked coaster.

> The ride goes fastest at the bottom of the hill because most of the potential energy has been changed into kinetic energy.

Full of Energy

Traditional roller coaster rides use a chain, powered by an electric motor, to haul the cars up the first and tallest hill. After that, the roller coaster travels the rest of the way all on its own! As the roller coaster is pulled up the first hill, it stores up a kind of energy called **potential energy**. At the top of the hill, that potential energy changes to **kinetic** (moving) **energy** as the coaster zooms down the hill.

After it passes the bottom of the first hill, the roller coaster begins to climb again. No more power is needed to keep the roller coaster going. As it goes up and down each successive hill, the roller coaster's energy keeps switching back and forth between potential energy and kinetic energy. The potential energy it has at the top of each hill changes to kinetic energy and then back again.

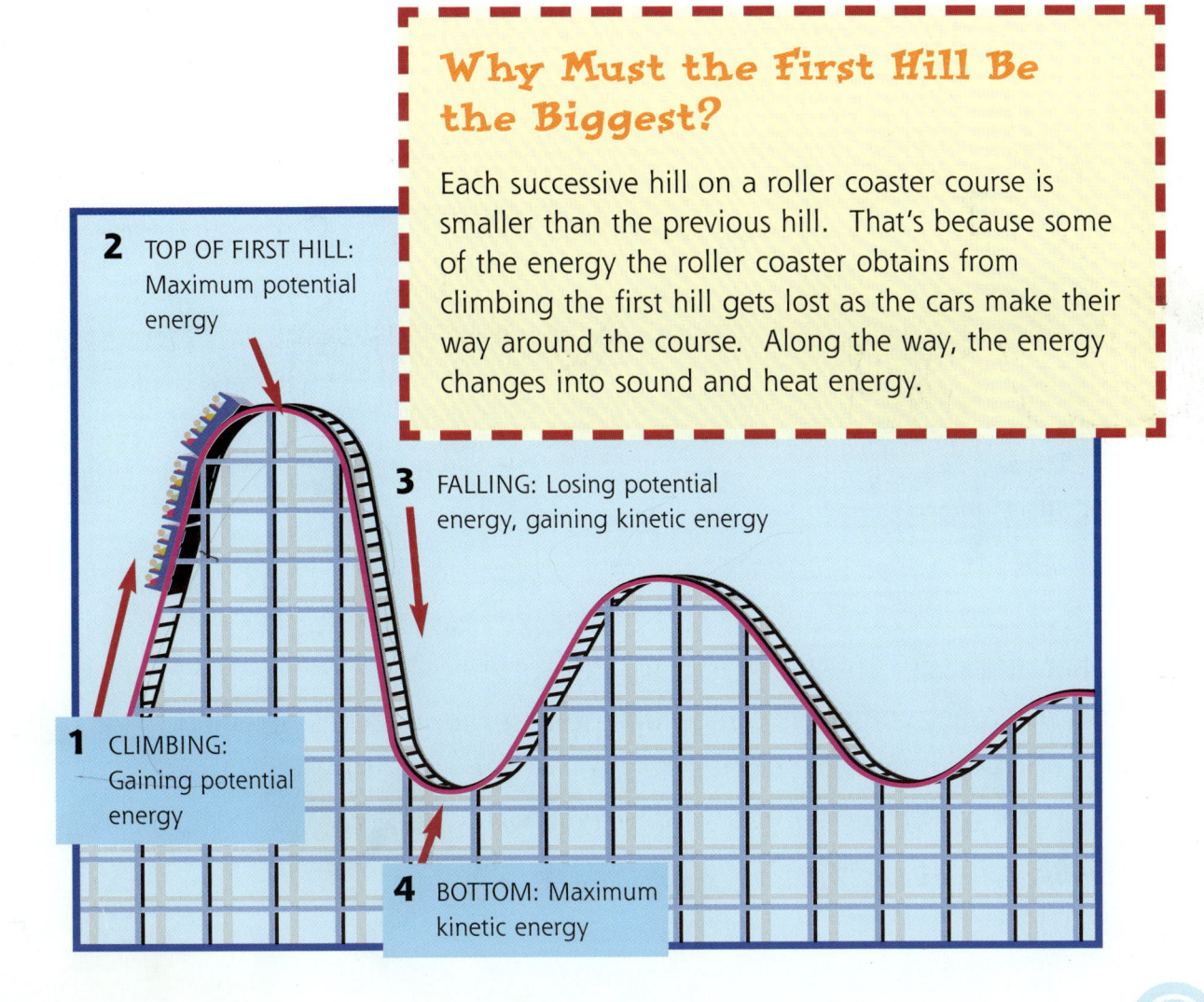

Why Must the First Hill Be the Biggest?

Each successive hill on a roller coaster course is smaller than the previous hill. That's because some of the energy the roller coaster obtains from climbing the first hill gets lost as the cars make their way around the course. Along the way, the energy changes into sound and heat energy.

1 CLIMBING: Gaining potential energy

2 TOP OF FIRST HILL: Maximum potential energy

3 FALLING: Losing potential energy, gaining kinetic energy

4 BOTTOM: Maximum kinetic energy

Some Classic Moves

As the roller coaster makes its way up and over the hills, some familiar forces are adding to the sensations you feel. The forces exerted on you by the track and the cars keep you pressed safely into your seat even as the car follows a hairpin turn.

Roller coasters have cars that are linked together like the cars of a train. Although riding in the lead car gives you the best view, it may not be as exciting as riding in the last car. As it starts down that first and highest hill, the lead car uses some of its energy to pull the other cars. The last car of the

One set of wheels guides the coaster on the track. Other wheels control side-to-side movement, and a third set of wheels is for safety when the cars are upside down.

roller coaster is the car that whips down the hills the fastest. It is helped by the weight and speed of the cars in front of it. The passengers toward the back of the roller coaster experience near-weightlessness as they soar down that first hill.

The Cyclone is a classic coaster famous for its nonstop action. Would you choose a seat in the front, the back, or the middle?

Riding the Big Coasters

It may be hard to imagine, but before 1976, no roller coaster featured loops. And now, if you take a look at a loop on any roller coaster, you'll see that it's an oval, not a perfect circle. To complete a loop that is a perfect circle, the cars

> Even when riders reach the top of the loop, they are still pressed into their seats. In fact, if they closed their eyes, they might not even know that they were upside down.

would have to travel very, very fast. At such high speeds, the riders would experience a force so strong that the riders would actually be in danger of passing out! Luckily, engineers discovered that the cars do not need to travel nearly as fast to complete an oval loop. Now, almost every amusement park features a roller coaster with loops. In fact, new roller coasters are able to do things that roller coaster designers of the past could only dream about. In 1997, Six Flags Magic Mountain opened a coaster whose design would have been considered impossible even a few years before. This scream machine is about 415 feet (126 meters) tall and can reach a speed of about 100 miles (160 kilometers) per hour.

Technology, working with the laws of motion that Newton discovered such a long time ago, will allow amusement park designers to offer you even more thrills in the years to come.

Forces at Play

A snowboarder starts by going down, then up. She continues over the slopes, making use of potential and kinetic energies in much the same way that a roller coaster does.

More Forces at Play

1 Now that you know about motion, take a look around you. Where do you see two objects about to exert forces on each other? What about centripetal force? Where do you see potential or kinetic energy?

(See page 30 for the answers.)

Longer supports allow a pendulum to swing higher. What would this girl be able to do if the chains on her swing were longer?

2 Think back to what you learned about bumper car collisions and weight. How could weight affect the outcome of the collision that is about to happen in this picture?

3

What type of force pulls the passengers toward the center of this ride?

4

As the boy takes off down the slide, his potential energy changes into what kind of energy?

29

Answers

1. Girl on a Swing
A playground swing is a lot like a pendulum. If the chains on this girl's swing were longer, she would be able to swing higher.

2. Soccer Player
In a bumper car collision, the lighter object is always going to feel the greater jolt. So, in the collision between the girl and the ball, the ball is going to feel the greater jolt.

3. Swing Ride
A centripetal force keeps the passengers moving in a circular path.

4. Water Slide
The potential energy he gained by climbing to the top of the slide changes to kinetic energy as he goes down.

Check out www.learner.org/exhibits/parkphysics/ where you can simulate bumper car collisions and design roller coasters as you learn more about amusement park physics.

Have a question about forces and the laws of motion? Log on to howthingswork.virginia.edu

Glossary

centripetal force: a force toward the center of a circle that causes an object to move in a circular path

energy: the capacity for doing work; forms of energy include kinetic, potential, sound, and heat energy

force: something that starts an object moving or that stops or changes an object's motion

kinetic energy: energy that an object has because of its motion

Newton's third law of motion: when one object exerts a force on a second object, the second object exerts a force equal in magnitude and opposite in direction on the first object

potential energy: energy that an object has stored because of its height above the ground

rotating: turning (in a circle) around an axis

reaction: an action in response to something that is happening

weightlessness: a sensation someone feels when he or she no longer feels the pull of gravity

Index

amusement park safety 4

bumper cars 6–9
  collisions 8–9
  laws of motion 9

carousel 11–13
  speed 13

centripetal force 12, 15, 30
  basketball 15
  carousel 12
  Ferris wheel 15
  swing ride 30

Ferris, George 14

Ferris wheel 11, 14–15

force 8–9, 28
  bumper cars 8–9
  soccer 28
  tennis racket 9

kinetic energy 22–23, 27, 30
  roller coaster 22–23
  water slide 27, 30

laws of motion 9

motion sickness 19

Newton, Sir Isaac 9

pendulum 16–19
  clocks 19
  parts of pendulum ride 18
  playground swings 28

potential energy 22–23, 27, 29, 30
  roller coasters 22–23
  snowboarding 27
  water slide 29, 30

roller coasters 20–27
  Cyclone 25
  loops 26–27
  tracks 24

third law of motion 9

weightlessness 19, 20, 25
  pendulum 19
  roller coaster 20, 25